A Special Book for You

Jovianna
From: Nana

I Love You!

Wherever You Are
my love will find you

Nancy Tillman

FEIWEL AND FRIENDS

NEW YORK

I wanted you more
than you ever will know,
so I sent love to follow
wherever you go.

It's high as you wish it. It's quick as an elf.
You'll never outgrow it . . . it stretches itself!

So climb any mountain . . .
climb up to the sky!
My love will find you.
My love can fly!

Make a big splash! Go out on a limb!
My love will find you. My love can swim!

It never gets lost, never fades, never ends . . .

if you're working . . .

or playing . . .

or sitting with friends.

You can dance 'til you're dizzy...

paint 'til you're blue. . . .

There's no place, not one,
that my love can't find you.

And if someday you're lonely,
or someday you're sad,
or you strike out at baseball,
or think you've been bad . . .

just lift up your face, feel the wind in your hair.
That's me, my sweet baby, my love is right there.

In the green of the grass . . . in the smell of the sea . . . in the clouds floating by . . . at the top of a tree . . . in the sound crickets make at the end of the day . . .

"You are loved. You are loved. You are loved," they all say.

My love is so high, and so wide and so deep, it's always right there, even when you're asleep.

So hold your head high
and don't be afraid
to march to the front
of your own parade.

If you're still my small babe
or you're all the way grown,
my promise to you
is you're never alone.

You are my angel, my darling,
my star . . . and my love will find you,
wherever you are.

To Daddy, whose love always finds me, wherever I am.

A FEIWEL AND FRIENDS BOOK
An Imprint of Macmillan

Feiwel and Friends books may be purchased for business or promotional use. For information on
bulk purchases, please contact the Macmillan Corporate and Premium Sales Department at
(800) 221-7945 x5442 or by e-mail at specialmarkets@macmillan.com.

Library of Congress Cataloging-in-Publication Data Available

ISBN: 978-1-250-08396-8

Book design by Nancy Tillman and Kathleen Breitenfeld

Feiwel and Friends logo designed by Filomena Tuosto

First Edition: 2010

10 9 8 7 6 5 4 3 2 1
mackids.com

Kohl's
Style: 1250083966
Factory Number: 123386
7/15-10/15

This special edition was printed for Kohl's Department Stores, Inc.
(for distribution on behalf of Kohl's Cares, LLC, its wholly owned subsidiary)
by Feiwel and Friends, an imprint of Macmillan Children's Book Group.

You are loved.

Nancy Tillman is the author and illustrator of the bestselling picture books, *On the Night You Were Born*; its companion journal, *The Wonder of You: A Book for Celebrating Baby's First Year*; *You're Here for a Reason*; *The Heaven of Animals*; *Wherever You Are, My Love Will Find You*; *I'd Know You Anywhere, My Love*; *The Spirit of Christmas*; and *The Crown on Your Head*. She also created the mischievous cat Tumford in *Tumford the Terrible* and *Tumford's Rude Noises*, and illustrated *It's Time to Sleep, My Love* by Eric Metaxas.

Nancy's mission in creating her books is to convey to children everywhere that "You are loved." She lives in Portland, Oregon. You can visit her online at the Nancy Tillman Corner at mackids.com and at nancytillman.com.